MW00952826

Dedication:

To my family:

For always believing in me and telling me to reach for the stars. Thank you for helping me to be the type of person I am today. Without you, I am nothing.

To my friends:

My first editors! Thanks for the honest critiques.

To my teachers:

Thank you for all the work you've done to shape me into the person I am, and thank you for helping me to mold my words into stories.

To everyone else:

You've all shaped a part of my life. For that, I am eternally grateful.

Table of Contents:

Laurie

Laurie

Laurie wears her hair the same way every day, half up, half down. Everything about her is indecisive; her lips partially creased, her eyes brightly glazed, her fingers loosely curled into a fist. She is immune to emotion, transparency, and change. When I first met her, she was 18 inches tall. She has not grown since, and she never will.

When I was seven, Laurie was one of my best friends. The compatibility between us was beyond words, as was our friendship. She always let me choose the day's adventure, never once objecting. That was what I liked about us: I never spoke, and she never spoke back. When she tired of the dress she wore, I picked out a new one for her. I brushed her hair when she'd slept on it too long, admiring the way it always shined, no matter how fierce the day's wind had been. I showed her how to drink invisible tea, to read and write the way I did, to speak without ever making a sound. She needed me.

I was always amazed at Laurie's ability to fall asleep at night. As long as she was lying down, her eyes remained closed; she never once woke up screaming. I, on the other hand, could not decipher the secret of slumber. It took me hours to drift asleep, and when I finally did, I was not really sleeping. I was awake, in my dreams. Earlier one night, I had listened to a familiar melody, hoping to trick my mind into letting its guard down so I could quietly seep under. Once I'd slipped, the music resumed inside my head, picking up right where it left off, though I knew that I had been awake to hear a long pause, a loud click, and more silence. But the continuous notes and their mystery were not what awakened me; these were a mere prelude, a

2

Laurie

misleading prelude to deceive me in my dreams. What came next was usually a nightmare.

I have been silenced and kidnapped by a dark shadowy figure who covered my mouth tightly with a cold, dark gloved hand. Another time I stared a murderer square in the eyes screaming "Why?! Why?!" then proceeded to beat him hysterically with a hand towel as he stood laughing at me through piercing eyes. And once, I fell from the sky. It was a brilliant night sky of the richest black, broken only by silver specks poking through the darkness that danced together, sparkling farther above me as I fell. I woke myself up in a cold swear, confused by the source of my fear. I hadn't screamed; no sound had come out. The stars would never have heard me. They were too far away. And if not, would they have listened?

The next night I dreamt that I was climbing a huge tree, so large that I could see neither the crest nor the trunk. All I knew was that I had to hold on tight. I could not fall, because I could not see the ground. I could feel the distance though, and it was a long way down. Suddenly, I realized I'd left Laurie on a branch just below me. Should I leave her? The thought crossed my mind, but did not linger.

Carefully, I stepped down to the branch beneath me, reaching to grab her hand. As I grasped the tiny fingers, I told her to take my hand and to hold on. But she could not accept my grip; her hand would not allow itself to conform to mine. She dropped, and I watched as she fell, staring down as guilt swept over me. She had not slipped - I had let her go. And now she was gone, lost in

3

Laurie

the black hole...I wondered if I could follow? Could I find her? Wind blows, a cloud appears beside me and I hear a voice repeat, "Escape."

I look below me; Laurie is gone. I look up and resume climbing toward an endless sky of shaky branches.

I sat up abruptly. I was wide awake. Beside my bed, Laurie was lying stiffly on her back on the floor. As I watched her sleep, I noticed that there was not a scratch or bruise on her. Out of the corner of my eye, I could swear that I saw her blink. I stare at her for minutes, studying her face, watching, waiting, expecting to catch her when she least suspects it. But she does not move. She is inanimate, I, inadequate, and envious. I turn over, close my eyes, and dissolve into a long, empty sleep.

Holiday Melancholy

Holiday Melancholy

The cold outside was too much to bear. What was a beautiful blanket of white to the people inside was a deep sheet of suggesting death to the girl. She was not much of a girl, small for lack of food, but strong for many miles walked on tough, calloused feet. Anywhere that there was warmth, if in small measures, or shelter, was home to her. Today she found herself in a rural area, which was much more forgiving than the lonely streets she had grown on. She didn't know where was, why, she didn't even know who she was. Her age was known to no-one, and neither was her smile. Maybe because it had rarely crossed her face, maybe because it was rarely given reason to. And maybe because, when you live wherever you can find a potential temporary shelter, you just don't smile often.

Most people at this time of year would be celebrating, putting out decorations like Christmas trees or menorahs, baking delicious-smelling pies and cookies and other foods that the girl could only dream of tasting.

The holidays did certainly get people in a better, more giving mood. But it also gave the girl great reason to envy the people who had a place to sleep and meals to eat, and, in general, people who had lives worth anything. She'd curl up somewhere, with only her worn pants and shirt, and the large brown jacket that had been coat, blanket, floor, roof, and wall to her. And she'd watch the people. She watched the kids play in snow, and the parents sitting on the porch, and the old grandparents rocking in chairs, and the amazingly innocent babies wrapped up many times, their new-to-the-world cheeks

Holiday Melancholy

pink with chill. And she'd then close her eyes and smell, and she smelled wonderful things. Pine needles and sugar cookies, pancake breakfast and apple cider, chocolate and cinnamon and mashed potatoes and burning wax, and fires, and pies, and just-before-snow. And her sense of feeling was sensitive, to cold and warm, and burn and dew.

Tonight the girl walked across a snow-buried farm that seemed dragged down by the night, blue and drab and mysterious. A handsome brick farmhouse that looked so welcoming kept drawing the girl to it.

"Come, girl," it said, "I keep this family warm. I can keep you warm." Her eyes and body were tired, so she gave in to weakness and walked toward the house. She was good at staying invisible. She found a dark corner of the house and decided that it was the best place to stay for the night. The corner was secluded enough that for once the girl didn't have to burry her hands into the snow and make herself as small as possible. She took out an old blanket with a worn pattern of brown and green and blue plaid, and she spread it over the white, crunchy snow that chilled her blood. She huddled all up, hoping to find warmth somewhere inside her own body. And she wrapped the huge jacket around herself. From the inside of a deep pocket she pulled out a half loaf of bread. It was all she could get with her begging money that would last awhile. She bit into a slice. The bread was as dry as a bone, and it made the girl cough out cold air. Oh, it was so cold. The girl pulled her numb legs closer to her chest, and she decided that tonight she would die her silent death.

Holiday Melancholy

The girl's eyes slowly opened. They blinked around, and she realized: she had survived. Another cold night she had survived when she probably shouldn't have. An unforgiving layer of frost covered everything, including the girl. The evergreens stood proudly, un-rustled by winds and untouched by humans. The girl peeked around through unbelievable gold-hued eyes. It was light out, and probably time to be moving on. She collected herself and stood up. She walked around back to where the dirt roads were and, before leaving her sleeping place, looked back. There was a menorah in the window and the rest of the house was glowing. She walked on, ready for another meaningless day of walking on her thick feet, slumping on the streets begging for change, watching all the people in their festive holiday activities, and once again finding a somewhat remote spot to sleep at night.

Speeding cars swished by, a bad idea on such thick ice. Cold water splashed at the girl's feet. An occasional person would drop whatever few cents they could find at the bottom of their pockets. The lights of the city gleamed like the stars she saw in the country. Another night had fallen.

The girl roamed the streets aimlessly, and found a dark, dirty alley to lie down in. She pushed a trash can away and curled up against a graffiti covered wall. Shivering, she remembered when she used to wish for a new life, to start over and change the world. Now she just wished for food and warmth and someone who loved her enough to spend the holidays with her.

Ice

Ice

The traveler walked across a vast frozen lake. How far across was the lake, and how wide? The traveler did not know. There was a visible path across the field of ice, tracks of those who came before him. Aside from this, there was little evidence proving that he was not, in fact, the only person on earth. Every so often he would chance upon a garment. A scarf caught by the wind, mittens, boots or even a coat cast aside, perhaps by mistake, perhaps by chance, perhaps by madness. The traveler cherished these relics, and added them to his own person. Valuable allies in this bitter war against the never-ending cold of this place. Wherever this was. Sometimes the traveler would stop and turn around, facing the direction from which he came. Memories of his origins were dim, and he could no longer remember why he had decided to make the journey. Many times he attempted to trace his path in his own mind, judging from the path behind him, but the sun was forever concealed behind clouds, and the tracks were obscure. The traveler could see a short way both behind and in front, but he dared not turn back, for there must be a reason for coming all this way (what?), and the way ahead frightened him, for he knew not what lay in the future, and the tracks ahead were disorienting. The decision to follow the path made by others came almost instantly, when he first saw it. Almost. That moment's hesitation worried him sometimes. But for the greater part, he trusted in the path. For, he reasoned, since others have obviously come this way with no evidence of trouble, the

Ice

ice must be safe to cross. He continued with the belief, the hope, that at least one of their number was certain of the destination, and could explain to him the reason of the journey, which he had forgotten. But he had to find those others first.

As he traveled he passed the time wondering what the other people were like. *Were they friendly? Were they hateful? Were they as lonely as he himself was?* He had known people before, he was certain of it. He had only brief sketches of memory, but that was no great matter. He would soon find others. For in truth he was very lonely, as anyone would be who walked endless days and nights in such an arctic desert. The only sound he heard was that of the wind. On the times that he rested he sat listening to the wind, and if he listened long enough and close enough he sometimes fancied that he heard voices, carried through the eternal twilight by a maverick chill wind. At these times, sometimes inside of him exploded to the surface, and he found himself calling out strange words, strange names, to people he did not know, to people that may or may not exist. Then the voices would be still. When the wind picked up again it carried back only bitter laughter, and he would fall asleep with that sound in his ears.

As he walked he noticed that the great path he followed was in truth many smaller paths and that while each set of tracks before him followed the same general direction, each seemed to get there in its own way. Some of the sets of footprints followed a fairly straight course,

Ice

and others made strange spiral designs or made wild turns or doubled back on themselves for any number of unfathomable reasons. He had always followed one straight path, as it seemed less confusing and more sure of itself. He noticed, in passing, that whoever had made the straight paths had little regard paths and markings of others nearby, even going so far as to destroy someone elses path to proceed. The traveler thought that this was rather sad.

One day, something astonishing took place. He was following the same straight path that he had followed for time uncounted, when that path suddenly came to and end. It simply ended, with that last footprint, and went no further. With no footprints to follow, the traveler was at a loss. He had never encountered an obstacle such as this before. Not knowing what else to do, he simply sat and pondered his next course of action. There must be action. He could not sit forever. Where there was no action there was death, and with it the end of the journey. To many unanswered questions. He sat like this for a long time, turning the situation over in his mind many times.

Finally, he decided that there was only one possible action he could take, however alien the idea might be. He would follow another path. So he came to his feet and, selecting from the nearby paths the one that seemed straightest and most direct, went on his way. He had not gone long, however, when this path, too, came up short. The traveler was perplexed, and grew anxious.

Ice

This was the second time his chosen path and ended abruptly. Trying to quell his anxiety, he reasoned to himself that perhaps the makers of these paths had chosen to follow someone else's path. *But why would they do this?* he thought.

Slightly unnerved, the traveler chose yet another path, straightest of those remaining. This, too, ended without explanation. Truly concerned now, the traveler chose path after path, more frantically each time, all with the same result. Until at last, in utter despair, the traveler broke down and wept. What kind of person will make a path for another to follow, claiming to know the way but all the time lying to himself and those who follow, ultimately disappearing altogether?

The traveler wept for many days. He had based his course on a lie, an unfounded belief. He had followed his chosen path faithfully, never leaving, never deviating. He had not left the path; the path had left him. And now he was lost. He cried. In the extreme cold his tears crystallized before the touched the ground. Sorrow and anguish, emotions frozen forever in time. His tears took the sadness with them, leaving him with a disappointed anger.

He leapt to his feet, cursing in full voice the powers that brought him to this place. This oh so cold wretched frozen hell. He remembered that there were other paths to be followed. Not straight paths, no. He would follow a winding path this time. Perhaps the maker of those paths had once entertained these same

Ice

thoughts, forsaking the straight sets of footprints for those that seemed instead to wander all across his field of vision. He did not know. He would not find out. He walked. In time he came to notice that the many twisted paths he came across where all, in fact, the same path only at different points.

Much time passed, and still the winding path did not end, but the traveler found himself beginning to doubt the course. It seemed to him that the path wound across the land in elaborate circles and loops, so that he did indeed travel uncounted hundreds of steps but could still plainly see the place where he had first joined the path! He thought this to be somewhat ridiculous, but that part of his main was overshadowed by a greater part that wished to follow the path regardless, only because there were no alternatives. He walked the only winding path, and the straight paths always ended quickly. So he continued to follow the winding path, slowly making progress toward the destination that he could not see. He walked for hours, days, weeks. He could not tell how long, and he did not care. The path continued. Suddenly it bothered him that the path could stretch on so far, seeming to have no end. He became more frantic as he walked. Anxiety and despair pushed him forward, quickening his blood. He responded by quickening his pace. He moved from a brisk walk to a steady jog, and when this did not satisfy his faceless fears he pushed harder, until he was running, running as only a desperate man knows how. Now, it so happened that he was

Ice

running so hard and so fast that he did not see the end of the path until his forward foot was already coming down hard onto the patch of ice directly ahead of the last footprint. He felt a split-second of alarm just before his foot hit the ice, and then CRASH!

He barely cried out before the docile surface of that endless lake turned against him, opening it dark jagged maw to swallow him whole. The water was deep, and it was dark, and it was deathly cold. A merciless chill unlike any he had felt before took hold of him; this demon in fluid form assaulted his body at every point. His many warm garments did nothing to keep the cold away. The chilly waters mocked him. Did he dare to believe that things like warmth and life, things so fragile and finite, could overcome this heartless opponent, a cold that brought darkness with it, a cold that slept beneath the arctic ice, a cold that ruled the places beyond the last start, the cold that was here first of all and would always remain?

He did not hesitate. He walked through. He was totally unprepared for what he found here. He stepped through the door into the middle of a large grassy field. it was warm and the sun was shining brightly. A light breeze blew across the field, not spitefully tossing powdery snow into his eyes but playfully blowing through the tall grass, creating a flowing ocean of green and blue and gold near the horizon. This was summer. He knew this. It was wonderful. The sights, the smells, the warmth, the sounds. The sounds? In the distance he

Ice

still heard waves crashing angrily, but another sound, much nearer, caught his attention. It was the sound of children laughing. He ran through the tall grass with a pounding heart. And he came to a great clearing in the middle of the field. There he saw the impossible. It was a farmhouse. And beside that, a barn. The smell of a baking pie floated on the light wind. He wrapped himself in it. In the small yard in front of the house there stood two small children, one boy and one girl, no more than five years old each.

They looked up at him with their wide eyes and innocent faces. And they smiled. Come play with us! they cried. He took a step forward, and was suddenly hit with the surprise feeling of being caught within a very small space. He looked around him, at the darkness on the horizon, and it did indeed seem as if the walls of this world were closing on him. The blackness followed him even here. This place was the last. The eye of a monstrous hurricane that would eventually be consumed as everything else had been. The horizon was black on all sides, a chill wind arouse around him. He thought then of the children. He couldn't let them perish in this storm.

"Go!" he shouted to them. "Run away! Run away before it catches you or you will die!"

They did not move. Instead, they smiled at him again, and, somewhat to his surprise, he smiled back.

"Silly!" the little boy said. "You can't run from that."

Ice

"Silly!" the little girl repeated. Nobody dies.

The children came to him, and he gathered them in his arms. He held them up, one in each arm. The little boys arms wrapped around his neck, and the little girl kissed him on the cheek. Together they faced the coming darkness, that dreaded implacable cold, and they laughed.

*****

The traveler pulled himself out of the frigid water and set to making a fire. When he was once again warm and dry he decided to continue his journey. He looked around at the great collection of paths that stretched from one end of the world to the other, east to west and west to east. The traveler laughed aloud and found his strength returning.

I will not take the straight path or the winding path, he thought, *for both were made by others, and they will take me nowhere. The only path I shall walk is the one I make for myself.*

And with that the traveler promptly turned and started walking southward, thinking of pies.

When the World Cried

When The World Cried

Looking back at it, she knew it changed her life forever. Nothing would ever be the same ever since that horrible day. A day that would definitely go down in American history books. Something her children would learn about and ask her about because she would remember. It was something she lived through, though at times she felt so guilty for living when so many people died that day.

She hit every emotion that day and the days following. She didn't miss one of them. Her day started with fear, followed by terror. The she hit shock, and bewilderment. Later on came the numbness and grief. She hit despair when the phones wouldn't dial out, and exhilaration when they did. She felt joy days later when she was able to speak to her loved ones on the phone and hold her loved ones in her arms once again, and gut wrenching pain as she stood and watched the other caskets close.

She felt the joy when she held her godson in her arms. When she felt his need for love and caring, she felt immeasurable sorrow and pity when he cried out for his mother and father, who were never to return. She knew she could not be both his mother and father. She could be neither. She knew that the baby would grow to cherish the memory of his parents, and to cherish all that life would give to him. He was a miracle baby after all. He was wanted and loved by so many people, including her.

In her heart that day, she knew she would be alone

When The World Cried

in taking care of her godson. His godfather was overseas in the military and would not be willing to come home, nor would he be willing to become a father. He did not want a family. She phoned the babys godfather and began to cry. She was so young, and she didn't want to go through this alone. He tried to console her from a long distance, but it didn't work. She kept crying because she was so alone, with an eleven month old child, and far from the place and people she called home. She was stuck there, with a baby, by herself and didn't know what to do.

That day she watched in horror as people jumped from buildings and scrambled to save their own lives and the lives of others. She felt immeasurable pride in the nation binding together, for people of different races, creeds, national origins and religions selflessly giving of themselves and helping out their fellow man. She knew there would be many unnamed heroes, and many unrecorded acts of kindness that would take place that day. She wondered how many people would not have escaped those towers if they had not been helped by a complete stranger.

Today looking back on that day and the following weeks, she realized that life is never so bad. There are miracles that happen every day, there are people who know the meaning of helping other people. She realized she possessed a strength deeper that she could have ever imagined. She knows the value of family and the bonds that can be formed with or without blood ties. And she

When The World Cried

knows that family is not always biological, but it is a feeling, love can be felt for anyone, regardless of blood relations.

Every night now, she goes to bed happy with the life she led that day. She doesn't take things for granted anymore. When she says "I love you" she means it, and she will always make the time in her life to tuck her godson in just a little tighter, and to hold is hand and be there every step of the way as he grows up. That day she entered life as a child, and closed that day a woman. She stands by her family through everything and knows now, that in times of hardship, they will stand by her too.

Remembrances

Remembrances

She walked into the hospital with a slight quiver coursing through her body. Hospitals are a frightening place to be, either if you are sick or if you are just visiting. The smell of antiseptic invaded her nose like an army conquering the enemy in battle. Her nose fought to keep the smell of the flowers blooming outside the hospital, rather than submit to the disinfectant that all hospitals seemed to use. Her ears rang with the pain as the silence was broken by nurses walking about in their rubber soled shoes and as a crash cart suddenly began squawking. She quickened her pace and found the nearest elevator to take her up to the third floor.

She knew exactly where the room was she needed to visit, yet she walked in circles around the wing, just thinking. She had been to that room a thousand times before, it had become like second nature to her. Spotting a seat near the nurses station, far enough away from that room for now, she sat and put her head between her hands. Her head was thinking a thousand things all at once, and running a mile a minute, yet her concentration was on none of them; only the words she remembered so clearly. They echoed like a clap of thunder in a canyon during a storm. Over and over, those few words kept repeating themselves. *Why couldn't they just go away?* They were still her inspiration; they always would be, but times are different now. She still needed the words, just not in the same way.

Life wasn't about getting everything that you want. She found that out the hard way. Sometimes, the

Remembrances

things that are the least expensive matter the most and it took a long and difficult battle to figure that out. She leaned back in her chair and sighed deeply. Maybe life isn't always fair, but if you remain true to yourself everything will turn out okay.

That was a time that she wished she could say the things that she'd wanted to, to the people she wanted to, but she was never sure how to put what she thought and she never knew just when to say exactly what she felt. After the events of the last few years, she realized that she had to seize the day and never take anything or anyone for granted again. Now, she just says what she feels, when she feels it. If she didn't say what she felt, then she would be giving into all the pressures put forth by society. Her life was worth so much more than that; she couldn't let them win that easily.

Slowly she stood up and began a slow walk to the room she needed to enter. She knocked gently on the door, and a soft voice answered, "Come in."

She walked into the room and smiled a broad smile. Her eighty year old mother was sitting on the edge of the bed, with a knapsack zippered at her feet. She could hardly tell that the woman sitting on the bed was the same woman who, three months ago, suffered a severe stroke. She walked over to the woman, helped her to her feet and into the waiting wheelchair.

"Its time to go home Mom."

With that, they left the hospital and went out into the beautiful spring day that held the promises of so

Remembrances

much more.

Emma's

Heart

Emmas Heart

The snow was falling in small, circular waves, coloring the wind white. Emma knew that it would continue to trap her in all night, continue to tease her with serenity that she longed for as it blanketed the darkness in white, crystalline tidbits of frost. It was so cold outside, cold enough to freeze her thoughts so she could trap them like stunned fish in a frozen lake and lay them out before her, flapping scaling diction. She looked up at the lightbulb as it flickered impatiently casting stagnant shadows on paper as cold and white as the night outside.

That morning she had stared up at her ceiling, at the thick layer of dust that draped the tired arms of the fan as it stared down at her, lonely and useless in her cold room. Emma's neck hurt from the night before, from the straining upward to kiss impatient lips. She had lain in bed like that for hours, smelling her sweat, smelling his smell as it mingled with the tears that fell down her cheeks onto cloudy pillows. She had promised him it wouldn't mean anything, as the windows grew warm and clouded with fog on that rainy night. She had promised him it wouldn't complicate things, as she ran her finger along his earlobes and twisted his hair in her fingers hoping never to let go.

She had lied.

Now she sat alone, as flake fainted upon flake, avoiding the inevitable freezing over of wet tears and

Emmas Heart

saturated words. She knew that he vacancy, the desire she had for his strong arms to caress her shoulders, her hair, the curve of her thigh, the achings of her soul, would not make him any closer than the snow that fell outside, hidden from her by the transparency of the window, the heat of woolen blankets, the flicker of lit bulbs.

Emma melted into oblivion as the world around her froze with the impending night, as the snow piled up outside of her door, as the dust on her ceiling fan silently and patiently gathered Emma's dying hopes and words as they flew with waxen wings, closer and closer to the unforgiving sun.

Leaving

Leaving

"I'm leaving tomorrow," I sort of pushed those words out of my throat, yet I could still feel them there. Waiting for his reaction, I pretended not to look at him as he studied the way my face fell with those words. He nodded solemnly, his lips tightly pressed together as he searched for something to say, some memorable words that I could carry on with me, for the rest of my life.

"I..," he began but paused again. I looked at him, trying to grasp every moment of his presence; to soak in it.

"I knew you were leaving," he tried to sound so sure, so strong. I remembered again exactly why I loved him.

He spoke again, "When I heard you were leaving- I guess I just didn't realize that it was real, that you were never coming back. I guess it wasn't real to me, ya know?"

"Yeah.. I know," I whispered back at him. Nervously putting a strand of hair behind my ear, "I've never been so scared my life," I said with a nervous laugh following. He smiled at me, kicking the dirt under his feet with his shoe. "But, I'll be okay -" I tried to reassure myself.

He smiled at me with the same wide eyed look he always had, the one that never had failed me before so I was reassured slightly.

"Yeah, you'll be okay."

I loved the way his lips curved and moved with those words. From the look in his eyes at that moment, I

31

Leaving

knew exactly what had drawn me to him.

"You're always okay, remember?" He chuckled slightly. I could tell that he didn't want me to leave him.

"Always.." I smiled at him again with those words, then again studied that exact expression on his face, the same one I had fallen in love with so many years ago.

A silence grew between us- the eerie silence when you can hear each breath and every beat of your heart. I couldn't find the words to say. For the first time in my entire life I was speechless. At this point we had both known that I was really leaving. This time this really was goodbye.

Mountains of memories built up inside my head and I began to realize that this could be the last time we'd both be sitting here together alone, and that yesterday might have been the last time we'd spend sitting for hours sipping cappuccino at our favorite local café. I didn't talk for those few awkward moments of silence. I stood there enjoying his presence. I had no idea when or if I'd ever see him again.

Feelings of loneliness crept inside my insides, and that is when it occurred to me that for the first time in almost five years I wouldn't have his arms to comfort me every time my hear was broke. He wouldn't be there to reassure me that everything would be okay, or even to tell me that I had bad taste.

I began to wonder if those were the things he'd miss about me. For nearly five years of my life I've had this remarkable friendship and now it's slipped through my fingers.

Leaving

"I think you'll do what you've always done," he said.

"What's that?" I asked curiously.

"You'll get out of bed, you'll do so well, go to an exciting new place, you'll smile, laugh, make some great new friends, and date guys that don't deserve you."

I smiled softly at him with salty tears multiplying down my face- one by one creating a waterfall from my eyes.

"Don't cry babe," he put his arms around me, lifting me from the ground, like he has always done. His strength was my weakness.

As we stood face to face I knew that it was over. That our time together was limited, that I had to say good bye to probably the best person I have ever had the privilege of knowing, of being friends with. I knew the bond we had would never be broken.

We said our good byes and we walked away from each other. I will never forget my whole life how the back of his head looked as he walked away from me, and for the first time in my life, I was alone. But he will always be in my heart.

Summer

Wind

Serenade

Summer Wind Serenade

The dirt under Summer's feet rose up in smoke as she tread upon it. This was the longest walk of her life. She dreaded coming home.

"I hope nothing happens," she whispered miserably, dust still rising in billowing clouds under her. She continued kicking at the dust and finally saw her home. She hoped her father wasn't there.

As she walked up to the door, it opened, and there he was, looking at her. Summer screamed inside her mind.

"Come with me," he said, and walked ahead of her. He led her to her room and told her to sit down.. He stood in front of her, holding her leather book with Kokopelli engraved on the cover. It was her diary. A complete years worth of her deepest secrets, dreams, and hopes in love. Summer, trying not to acknowledge it, looked at the carpet.

"Go to your mat," was all she heard her father say, and he said it softly. He then walked away and left. That was it. And he had left her diary on the mat, right beside her. She opened it, curious, wondering what he had read, though she knew he had ready so many bad things. There was Luke, Coyote, the New Moon and so many things. Even what happened with her best friend, Leila. Summer just read the last page. It was dated last month.

'Dear Diary,

Summer Wind Serenade

Today, yes today is the day I forgot Luke. Leila knows nothing about him and I'm not going to tell her either. I don't want her to know. Yes, she knows who he is, but still! I'm not telling her. Its none of her business....'

Summer closed her eyes. Luke. She still remembered him. Like the beauty of the sunset and the sparkling morning dew, he captured the beauties of Earth and teased Summer's eyes with the gorgeous splendor. And yet, she still remembered that day. Because it was that day, that very day, that she regretted forever.

*****

"Summer!"

Summer turned around and saw her boyfriend, Coyote running after her. She giggled. The way he ran was so loser-like! He had the body of a skeleton and it wouldn't be surprising if his body rattled also.

"Summer! Wait up!"

He finally caught up, his face flushed, he was clutching a small box wrapped in paper with a large maroon ribbon on top. He smiled, and held it out to her.

"I got this for you. It's for the ceremonies."

Summer smiled back at him and held it in her hands. It was light.

"Thanks a lot, you're so sweet! I have a gift at my house.. will you come with me to get it?"

36

Summer Wind Serenade

His eyes grew wide and he blushed. "You mean..back to your house? As in, inside?" he asked.

"Of course, come on. I have dance practice at six!" Summer said. "If I don't hurry, you'll make me late!"

With that, Summer began walking, Coyote still running to catch her. As they neared her house though, she noticed something. A large wagon was parked down her street. She watched curiously, Coyote still rambling on about what he thought she had gotten him. And that's when she saw him.

"Oh my God, he gorgeous....." Summer whispered to herself.

Coyote didn't even notice her speak, or how her eyes glazed over so suddenly. But Summer continued staring at the boy in front of the adobe house. The only adobe house in the neighborhood... vacant until now. Now he lived there. She didn't know his name, but he was beautiful. The most beautiful thing she had ever seen, but already knew Leila probably wouldn't think he was cute.

"Oh my God, Summer! The men you go for!" she could hear Leila now. Yes, that's definitely what she's going to say to me, thought Summer.

When they got to Summer's house, Coyote waited at the front door so as not to break her fathers rules about a boy being in the house, while Summer got his gift from inside. It was a new tortoise shell rattle for the ceremonies. Yet, Summer despised the tortoise rattles.

Summer Wind Serenade

She preferred the rainsticks. It was wrapped, yes, but when Summer went outside to give it to him, she glanced down the street.

I wonder what his name is, she thought.

"Thanks, sweetheart. You're an angel," she heard Coyote say.

But Summer continued looking down the street, and just nodded. When she went to her room, she lit some candles and got out her diary. It was a gorgeous leather book with the Kokopelli engraved on the front cover and trimmed with rabbit fur. Leila had gotten it for her and given it to her yesterday. The first thing she thought about writing was not Coyote, but of the mysterious boy who moved in down the street. The boy who moved into the adobe house.

*****

"Just write what your heart tells you, Summer!" Miss Long Tree said, entirely exasperated.

"But it doesn't tell me anything! My life is dull!" Summer responded. She knew everyone was looking at her, but she didn't care. Miss Long Tree sighed and looked out of the window of the classroom.

"Well, write about the weather, Nature, or something! Please Summer, don't make me fail you this semester. This is the only class you need to pass before they'll accept you into the Indian School for Teachers. You know it's mandatory that all Indians pass English!"

Summer Wind Serenade

and then Miss Long Tree walked away, sighing once more.

I don't feel anything, Summer thought, *and the weather is horrid! Who wants to hear about plants dying and animals sleeping?*

After five minutes of staring blankly into space, she looked up and Miss Long Tree was still watching her, biting her lip in worry. Summer, with a loud and long sigh opened her notebook. It was the first day back from the winter break, and she hadn't gotten back into 'school mode' But still, she looked out of the window all the same.

"Oh how I loathe the white schooling and the mandatory classes they make us take. I wish one day we could go back to the old ways," she wrote. The she erased it. Miss Long Tree would hate that, she was just like Summer.

"The leaves lay dead on the ground
And so do I during this time of year..."

She giggled. How stupid! She looked outside to see what color the front yard had turned when she noticed something. She recognized the horse tied to the willow tree. It was a strange tan horse. He was taller than the other horses and more interesting and she couldn't place where she had seen it before. Then she remembered.

"It can't be," she whispered. Her heart began to

Summer Wind Serenade

beat in loud shots of fear. She crept slowly up to the window.

"Uh, Summer? Please get back to your seat, please," Miss Long Tree said. The class was staring. Summer didn't appear to be paying attention.

"Summer Wind! Please get back in your seat or I'll send you out!" she said severely, Miss Long Tree hardly ever used her entire name. Summer head her this time.

"Wait a minute, Miss Long Tree. I'm looking for inspiration and I am getting a good idea."

So she stood at the window, looking out at the front lawn. There he was. The boy she had seen two weeks ago. Her heart thumped so loudly she held her chest to hold it back.

And from her lips, she whispered, not noticing: "My heart beats when you are near. My body yearns for the knowledge of you. Yet you are a stranger to me. A stranger that I know from somewhere before. Come up here and meet me, and tell me that the love we feel is true..."

*****

"So Miss Long Tree got worked up again? What happened this time?" Leila asked, grinning slightly. A small apple laid in front of her, shining and untouched.

"Well, she just sat staring at me, freaking out. She kept shrieking 'Summer! Summer!' It was pathetic. She

Summer Wind Serenade

asked me what I said, and I said nothing. She said that I said a beautiful line of poetry and I was staring out of the window as if I were in a trance. And get this! She said that it rhymed!" Summer squealed excitedly.

Leila stared at her, her mouth hanging open. Her eyes were so wide, it looked like her eyeballs could have fallen out. She began to stutter.

"My God, You've never ever rhymed. Ever! I remember you trying to rhyme in the first school! Hopeless!" Leila exclaimed, and then she recited in mockery.

'Leaves pass by
I say hi
Water is cool
And so am I'

Both girls began to shriek in laughter.

"Do you remember what, what was her name again did? She almost died of laughter! That moment was priceless!" Leila giggled harder, tears beginning to stream off her face. Summer pressed her face onto the table trying to hide her red face and keep from laughing so hard.

"Well, that's what you get for being my teacher, I guess," Summer said after they had calmed down a bit.

"But to see Miss Long Tree like that? You should of seen her face. Now that was priceless."

Summer was listening to the sound of everyone laughing and talking all at once. It was lunch time, and daresay, Summer was a second year in the Indian school.

Summer Wind Serenade

Leila began to gossip when Summer noticed it. Her heart thumped wildly, and her forehead burned with fever.

"Summer?"

"Sweet drops of yourself, I do taste with dreamy ecstacy. You torture me with every move, so stop all motion and let me be."

"I love you," he whispered, stroking Summer's hair. Summer looked down and blushed. "From the first time I saw you, I knew you were the one. The one I would spend my life with. Please tell me how you feel," he said once more, his eyes searching hers.

"I knew you were the one too..." Summer added, "and I love you."

The boy held her closer and gently whispered in her ear, "Then stay with me forever. Love me gently as red as the rising sun. Spend forever with me. Eternity knows that you are the one."

I know that you are the one......
know that you are the one....
thatyou arethe one....
theone....
theone....
one....
....

The words echoed on and on. Summer looked up and when she looked back at him, he was gone.

"Summer!" she heard someone whisper, and the

entire world seemed to darken. Everything faded and then was gone.

"Summer!"

Summer opened her eyes, slowly. She was lying on a brown leather sack which supposed to be a bed. But still, that was some dream.

"Well, I don't know exactly what to do, I've never been trained for this, you know," the nurse announced to Summer. "But still, you seem pretty strange to me. I don't understand what you were doing. I mean, your friend dropped you off here, your eyes were wide open, and you kept rhyming every little thing. I wanted to tape your mouth shut."

Summer stared at her. It was all a dream. The nurse looked closely at her eyes.

"Are you taking any medication from the medicine man? He does not know what he is doing. He is keeping you from being well. A real doctor would make you better in no time," the nurse said, concerned. She leaned in closer to Summer. "I can't tell the signs of this. You should go into town and get a real doctor to check you out."

Summer looked all around her surroundings. The white medicine was lying everywhere. Totally gross, Summer thought. Our healers certainly aren't like this. She got up off the leather sack and began to walk out into daylight.

On her way out she saw him. Her heart pounded. The boy was sitting there, on one of the leather sacks,

Summer Wind Serenade

fixing an arrow. Summer had no idea what to do or what to say to the boy.

"Take a seat, I'll be right back," the nurse said, looking up at Summer. Summer looked down at the empty seat by him, and then sat. She immediately started to shiver.

How do I say hello, she wondered, and then it came to her. She could ask him the time, that's it. She could ask the most gorgeous creature on Earth the time. There he was, sitting, fixing his arrow. She could just ask him, and then that'll break the ice. *Yes! I'll do that*, Summer thought.

"Here's the name of a real doctor who may be able to help you," the nurse announced loudly as Summer turned bright red.

Then the tent flap opened, and Leila was standing there, gasping loudly. Her eyes wide with fear. "Are you okay?" she asked.

"Yes, I'm fine," Summer said, sneaking a glance at him to see if he was watching. He was still fixing that arrow.

"You really scared me, Summer. You have no idea how hard my heart was pounding! I was very worried about you!"

"I think I might have some sort of idea," Summer responded, as they left.

*****

Summer Wind Serenade

Dear Diary,
I still wonder what his name is. I saw him today
in the nurse's tent. I planned to talk to
him..honest! Well, it didn't go as I wanted. I
mean, I didn't have the chance.

Summer paused writing and stared at the wall of
the tipi. She dropped her quill, and laid on her back,
looking up at the opening in the tipi. The she sat back up
and continued writing.

Beauty envelops me
No longer pain, no longer misery
In him, I see so much perfection
I feel so strange, how can this be?

She closed her eyes, and began to think. Tomorrow, she
thought, tomorrow is the day. I'm going to say hello.

*****

"Good morning I say
To my good friend Summer,
She's the best poet in school, and
All morning, Miss Long Tree told us so"
"Shush," Summer said to Leila, feeling
embarrassed.
"Oh come on! She loves you now! She's been
talking about you all day! Everyone in the village

45

Summer Wind Serenade

knows!" Leila said, sitting down and putting out her lunch. Another shiny little apple. Summer wondered every day if it was the exact same apple from the day before. It probably was.

"She has me sit in the front row now," Summer sighed, "all because of my stupid trances."

Leila blinked. "But I wonder... why does it happen? Are you alright? Is it because of your mother?" she asked.

"That wasn't funny...the comment about my mother," Summer snapped.

"Sorry. But anyway, tell me! Whatever it is, you can tell me!" Leila pleaded, her eyes twinkling. Summer looked at her. *Maybe I should tell her*, she thought.

"Summer, I have to go gather some food for my family, but I will see you later. Here's my apple." Leila stood up, smoothed her skirts and walked away, her black hair shimmering down her back.

Summer poked at Leila's apple. I'm all alone now, she sighed, I guess I'll sit with Coyote. She picked up her notebook and walked to the tree. It was an old redwood, that had been standing ever since her grandfather was born. She saw him sitting, cross-legged, on the cold grass. As she approached, he looked up and smiled.

"Hey angel," he said, smiling at her.

"Can I eat with you today?" she asked.

"Oh sure. You know, I don't know why you don't do it everyday."

Summer Wind Serenade

Summer sat down, pulling her skirt lower to avoid everyone's stare. "Well," said Coyote, bringing back everyone's attention, "where's our food? He did say he'd be back in five minutes. Boy, I'm going to really get after him today."

Summer began to look down and think of her guy. She then looked at Coyote, her boyfriend. The boy with the scrawny body, annoying freckles, the silly grin, why didn't she notice it before? Then she saw him. She couldn't think. He was walking straight to her, holding several pouches of food. He wasn't looking at her at all though. "Finally!" Coyote shouts, "We're hungry!"

Summer looked at Coyote surprised. It couldn't be! she screams silently, mentally. But when the boy sat down across from her, her face flushed. *How can he not notice me?* she thinks, her heart racing off the grass and halfway to her home.

"Sorry, got caught up," the boy says, handing out the lunches. He gives short glances to everyone to make sure he gives them out correctly. Summer felt like she was about to scream, because that's when he saw her, really saw her. Her heart throbbed so loudly, she was sure that's why he was staring.

He's even more stunning up close. Please keep staring. Say something. Say hi. Hello. Good morning. I'm going crazy. How are you? I'm fine, thanks for asking.

Coyote looked at both of them and then at the boy. "Luke, you're going to clean up that mess, right?"

Summer Wind Serenade

Summer looked down and noticed that the boy had drenched himself in the contents of his lunch pouch, and the pouch was still in his hands, upside down. Her face blushed maroon as she pulls down her skirt, gets up, and goes to find Leila.

*****

"Summer, I'm incredibly surprised by you. You have vastly improved!" Miss Long Tree beamed.

Summer, still thinking about what happened earlier, muttered thank-you.

"Well, the reason I asked you after school is that, well there's a tribal dance competition along with poetry contest coming up, and I'd like to see your work in it. Really I would. Only the new stuff though, none of the old ones," she paused to smile, "Plus you'll get extra credit and there's a chance that you may get published! I would like you to enter into both of the competitions."

With that, she passionately threw both hands up. Miss Long Tree looked as if she was going to burst with happiness. Summer, on the other hand, looked less cheerful. "Well?" she asked, waiting still, her hands still hanging in the air.

"I suppose that I could," Summer replied looking dejected.

"Wonderful!" she shouted loud enough to wake up the dead. "See me tomorrow for more details. Be careful on your way home, the soldiers are still around."

Summer Wind Serenade

Summer tightened her cloak, and swore under her breath a few spells she remembered her grandmother teaching her. "I definitely should not have worn this skirt" she whimpers as the cold passes by, "and a poetry contest? How pathetic! The dance I can do, but poetry?"

On her way home, she began to sing. Wrapped up in the melody, she even added a few dance moves. She sang and sang and on and on she went. "This is my part," she smiled, and ended the song with the corniest smile and hand waving she could muster. To top it off, she bowed deeply. "Thank-you, thank-you," she muttered, smiling still. And in front of the adobe house at the end of the street he stood, frozen. "Oops," Summer whispered, looking down, her face maroon once more, "I forgot he lived there."

Summer ran inside her house, hoping he didn't recognize her. When she got to her mat, she peeked out the flap and he was finally going back inside. She had dance practice at sunset and a diary entry to write. What an incredibly lovely day, Summer thought bitterly. All this before supper.

The next day at school, Summer was in for the shock of her life. Miss Long Tree stood up and made an announcement. "I've uncovered some beautiful poetry! Just today! First hour, a student of mine unleashed it all! Dangerous thing, poetry, and that piece of writing could have been the end of me!" She held up a piece of paper as she continued. "Let me read it to you."

Summer Wind Serenade

"THE WORLD'S END

With deathful vengeance
I hear judgement's shriek
White horses of Death gallop by
Their coats so shiny, so sleek

Arrows are fired
Valleys are full
Floods strike bitterly
With the rage of a bull

Bong bong bong
The golden bell rings
From a sleek brown rope
Does that fateful bell swing

To fire our passion
Against world's end
A blessed life we share
As our fates inter-twine and bend

And here you are
Right by my side
Holding my hand
Against blood's tide

And I am content
Being here with you

Summer Wind Serenade

And as our beautiful world collapses
Whisper once more, that you love me too."

The class suddenly became hushed. Miss Long Tree looked around, a ridiculous smile on her face.

"Well? What do you think?" Miss Long Tree asked, still smiling. She then stopped looking around, and focused on Summer. Summer turned her head and shut her eyes, praying she'll stop staring. "Summer? What do you think?"

Summer looked up, knowing she couldn't evade the question. "Well... I thought it was good, and I'd really like to know who wrote it."

Miss Long Trees eyes grew wide in horror. She would never ever let anyone know that. She always kept this stuff anonymous.

"See me after class, Summer."

Summer groaned silently, and when the class was dismissed she tried to race out without Miss Long Tree noticing her, but she grappled her arm.

"Summer...Summer, Summer, Summer," she whispered excitedly, "I knew you'd want to know who wrote it! Top student, this person. Ahhh... I can hear you two now! Handing in the most gorgeous piece of poetry to that contest!"

Summer looked at the door. She could make a quick getaway right then. She felt like she was going to be sick.

"I want you to come here for lunch tomorrow.

Summer Wind Serenade

Two of my top student poets will conjure a masterpiece!"
she said, eyes twinkling.

*****

"Instead of glancing over there every single
second, why don't you sit with him?" Leila asks.

Summer looks up, "Huh? You know about him?"

Leila's eyes grow huge, "Of course, I know about
him! He's your boyfriend! I know how much you two are
in love; that's probably why you've been so good at
writing lately! All thanks to Coyote, your sweetheart!"

Leila grins. The tiny apple sits in front of her
again.

"It's not that," says Summer, still watching Luke.
Whenever he looked her way, she wondered if he was
watching her too.

Couldn't be, she whispers to herself. But there it
was again. Her heart was pounding against the table.

"So Miss Long Tree read a poem to us today.
About death. Did you write it?"

"No, I didn't."

"Oh, well, you're not the only poet in this school,
I guess...," Leila mutters. Summer began to sense
jealousy every now and then, but ignored it.

"I'm going to break up with Coyote," Summer
said suddenly. Leila looked at her.

"Seriously?"

"Yes."

Summer Wind Serenade

"But why? You two make such a great couple."

"Well, its been so long. I need to keep around, you know?"

Leila looks at the table and begins picking at it.

"Does that mean, does that mean... I can go for him now?" Leila asks, still not looking at her. Summer looks up, surprised.

"What do you mean?"

"You know exactly what I mean. I saw him first, but he saw you first, apparently. He was in my sixth grade class, I tried talking to him all the time, but he would blow me off, thinking I was just another girl. I saw how he looked at you the very first time. When I saw that look in his eyes, I felt like dying. But you're my friend, you know? And all I want is just for you both to be happy."

Summer looks away. She never knew.

"Why didn't you just tell me?" she whispers.

Leila doesn't say anything. Finally, she picks up her pouch and walks away.

*****

Something was wrong the very next day. Summer sensed something out of balance. All day, she was anticipating something... but what? She didn't want to face Leila at all today, and was actually glad she had to meet Miss Long Tree during lunch break.

When she walked into the classroom she saw

Summer Wind Serenade

Luke sitting there.

"Oh no," she whispered. Miss Long Tree was nowhere to be found. Summer stood by the door, looking out, waiting for Miss Long Tree to show up. Her palms were sweating, her heart pounding, and she kept brushing her hair with her hands, nervously.

Why is he here? She wondered.

And then she saw Miss Long Tree coming up the side of the road. "Ahh! Summer! How are you?" she calls out. She meets with her in front of the classroom.

"So Luke didn't show up, eh? The guy who wrote that poem I read today? The top student I've been raving about?"

Summers heart dropped into the pit of her stomach. Everything in her was throbbing. Her heart palpitated. Luke sat across from her, Indian style on the grass, and was busy writing.

Oh god, she thought, *I can't think.* She hadn't written much, and she could not show it to him to compare. That would be embarrassing. She looked at the ground and began tapping her feet. A few seconds into it, Luke began tapping his feet as well.

"Well!" Miss Long Tree said, "lunch break is almost over, so why don't you two switch papers and critique?"

Summers heart thudded against the walls of her chest. Not looking at him, she passed her notebook, and he gave her his. She immediately noticed his handwriting. His m's, in particular, looked like arches.

Summer Wind Serenade

Similar to the way the willow bends during a thunder storm with the wind blowing with gale force. She held her breath and began to read.

ONLY YOU

'At the sound of falling rain
The earth silently grins
The clouds roll on and on
Trees sway in the wind

Leaves streaming off the cedars
To fall and lie silently on the ground
Drips of snow slide off the sky
To cover the streets with sound

Black painted across the heavens
Pink painted across the horizon
As the white mountains disappear from view
So does the golden shining sun

And the stars blink and sparkle
Through dark clouds as gorgeous, so light
I think to myself, only you
Can perfect this beautiful sight'

~Luke Whitewater~

Summer stares at the poem. She is in complete

Summer Wind Serenade

awe. Luke is looking at her, waiting. His eyes meet hers, and he turns red.

"What do you think?" he whispers, his throat dry. He stops staring at her, and, instead, looks out of the window.

"That was gorgeous," Summer says sincerely. She still looks at him, and Miss Long Tree said it was time to go to the next class.

"I expect to see you both here after-school!" Miss Long Tree says, as they walk to their next class.

*****

After-school Summer goes back to Miss Long Tree's class, hoping that Luke was already there. She sees him and smiles to herself.

"Summer. Please take a seat," Miss Long Tree says. Summer sits next to him. "So, you two are my top students! Summer writes poetry mostly about love and beauty, Luke, you write well with death and hope. I expect something gothic, Vampire-ish. No blood please. Okay, I have a short meeting I must attend. Work together, and I'll see what you two conjure up when I come back."

She leaves the room, and Summers heart immediately stops. They are both silent, the boy and she, until he leans close to her. "Okay," he clears his throat, "I'll write something dark, and I'll let you read it and add on to it."

Summer Wind Serenade

Summer sits still while Luke begins to write. Totally clueless about what to say, she stares out of the window again. And out in the middle of the field is that beautiful tan horse.

"Is that horse yours?"

Luke doesn't pause, "Yes."

"Was it expensive?"

"No. Uhh... he's old. I just take good care of him and give him a lot of love."

"Oh," Summer says. She starts looking at the ground again, and notices that he's tapping his feet.

"You dance?" he asks after a few silent minutes.

Summer turns crimson again, remembering the other day. "Yes," she finally says.

"Well....you dance well," she hears him say, but her heart is pounding so loudly she can hardly hear him. Luke continues writing silently for about three minutes more, and passes the notebook to her.

"Flair"

'The aristocrat looks down at her
Eyes swinging side to side
His mouth opens grandly
To reveal and evil grin, so strange and wide

'The girl looks up in horror
At the count so ghastly white
As he leans down upon her,

57

Summer Wind Serenade

Her neck, he soon bites

And soon he takes her all
Her body, neck and soul
She submits herself to him
Wanting desperately to be given more, more and more

Forgetting who she is
Leaving the past behind
Looking to the future
With fate she has readily dined

And after, the man looks down at her
And the girl just smiles back
For she loved being the Count's
Tasteful midnight snack.'

When Summer finished, she smiled. Luke was already smiling at her, "Well?" he asks.

"I'm not quite sure this is what Miss Long Tree wanted...but it's not done yet!" Summer says, still grinning.

Miss Long Tree, when she came back, laughed at the poem, and allowed them to leave. And on the way home, the wind blew Summer's hair silently, as she sat in the front seat of a beautiful tan horses saddle.

The gray-haired nurse peers down at her, suspiciously. Summer has just woken up and jumps back.

Summer Wind Serenade

"What are you doing?" Summer shrieks. The nurse looks at her, eyebrows narrowing.

"Dearie, you've passed out again."

Summer looks around, it couldn't be. Was it all a dream? What happened with her and Coyote? How much of it was a dream? "How long have I been out?" Summer asks.

"All day. You came in this morning, and it's about one o'clock now. You wasted all day sleeping! You see what drugs do to you?" the nurse screams passionately.

Summer looks at her, silently. After a few seconds, she gets up and walks out.

*****

"Ah! Summer! Good to see you! You know, you passed out in my class! My class! Can you believe it?" Miss Long Tree shouts, Summer gazing at her sleepily.

It's after-school, and Summer has no idea if she's supposed to meet Luke there. Her heart pounded, she had been thinking about him all day.

"Miss Long Tree, could you tell me when I passed out?" Summer asks.

Miss Long Tree beams down on her. She opens her mouth to speak when Luke walks in. Summers heart races when she sees him.

"Ah! The fine poet himself!" Miss Long Tree smiles. Luke just blinks. "Well..I'd better go now! Another important meeting!" Miss Long Tree booms.

59

Summer Wind Serenade

She then opens the door and walks out, leaving Luke and Summer alone. Summer looks at Luke, who pulls out a black notebook with a picture of a skull and crossbones on the cover. He was so beautiful. After two minutes, she asked.

"What did we do yesterday? After-school... did we do anything together?"

Luke looks up from his paper, slowly. "I gave you a ride home because you were lying in the parking lot. You woke up half-way to your house."

Summer blushes deeply and Luke returns to his paper. I was lying in the parking lot? How odd! Summer thinks. "So..do I pass out a lot?" she asks.

"Yes." he says, "all the time...do you really take drugs?"

"No!"

"Good."

Summer begins to think. She loved the way he wrote. Just the way he sat. She saw beauty in it. She had never seen anything in the world so gorgeous. After a few silent minutes, Luke passes the notebook to her. Summer looks down and begins to read.

"THE DANCE"

'Will you teach me how to dance?
She whispers sweet and slow
The young man is taken back
Surprised she didn't know

Summer Wind Serenade

But still he holds her hands
Dipping her gently down
Trying not to think
How beautiful she looked right now

'I know what you're thinking, dear man'
She finally whispers in his ear,
'And for one night lets not be afraid'
She adds in a voice sincere

So he kissed her cheek softly
And gently stroked her bangs
But then that's when he saw it
Her mouths two white, crooked fangs

The woman just smiled
And whispered, 'now you know,
will you leave me here alone
And hate me, my kind, my soul'

For a moment the man paused
Unaware of what to do
He then opened up his mouth and smiled
He had thought for a moment, and now knew

'You shall be my queen
And we shall rule Transylvania'
They then lived on together

Summer Wind Serenade

The vampiress and Dracula'

Summer looks at it once more. It did need work, but overall, she didn't like the mood of the poem. It was too specific, how can the reader relate? It was the end especially that needed the most attention.

"Well, we don't need to use it, I guess we just need variety," he says, noticing Summer not saying anything, "Have you worked on the poem from yesterday?"

Summer looks at him, "It's in my journal at home."

"Good, but I think that we're still a long shot from First Place. Keep writing and I guess we'll get something." He then took his pouch and left.

Summer sat still, not moving. What just happened there? Wasn't he supposed to give her a ride home? "Oh well," she muttered, "I guess I'll walk."

*****

Dear Diary,
What an odd day, I was hoping he'd give me a ride home, but it didn't happen. I'm waiting for him to ask me out. It is wrong that I expect the most beautiful creature on Earth to give me a ride home? After I sacrificed all day, dreaming and thinking about him?
I'm sorry I don't write everything in here, I guess that's why there are so many loopholes in my

Summer Wind Serenade

life's story. Oh well, but its interesting, isn't it?
grin
I have dance practice now, so I'll be going ..
sigh .. yea, I need to write more poems for the
contest.. I really don't want to.

Summer put her pen down. She was still stressed and upset, but didn't want it to get to her.

"Why is everything slowing down?" she asks, she felt like crying. She had no idea why.

*****

"I'm glad you're actually spending extra time with me," Leila says, "I hardly see you anymore."

Summer looks down, school just ended and she didn't want to stay after. She was too scared. And so now she sat with Leila at the well, doing nothing.

"Well, it's only a few minutes, but hey, it means a lot to me," Leila adds, digging in her bag. She pulls out something and holds out her hand. "Here."

Summer looks at Leila's hand. *Was it an apple?*

"Just take it."

Summer takes it and gasps. It was a cigarette. "What the hell, Leila!" she shrieks quietly.

"Oh come on, stop being a baby!" Leila whispers, sounding annoyed, "You need to grow up." Leila then lit up the cigarette in her hands and puffed silently. Summer couldn't believe it. But then she looked down.

Summer Wind Serenade

Do I have to grow up? she wonders, staring at Leila and then at the cigarette in her hand. Her father was always telling her to grow up. And when her mother was alive, she did the same thing. Was this what it was to be grown up? Without thinking, she put it between her lips.

"There you go," she heard Leila say, and she leaned back, allowing Leila to light it.

This'll do it. I'll forget everything. Coyote, Luke, Miss Long Tree....everything.

Summer breathed in silently and out. She coughed a few times when it caught up in her nose, but other than that, she thought she did pretty good.

"So are you going to tell me?" Leila asks.

Summer looks at her. *Tell her what?*

"Are you going to tell me why you've been acting strange?"

Summer looked at the street. "I don't want to talk about it."

"Forget you then."

Summer couldn't believe it. *What was happening to her friend?* They sat there silently for the rest of the time, watching people walk by when she saw him. Summer's heart pounded and pounded, on and on. He just passed by, not looking, his head down.

*****

"Have you ever danced with the devil at the pale

of moonlight?"

"I'm sorry, Summer. I'll never do it again."

"Yea, you pass out all the time." "Two of my top students will conjure a masterpiece!"

"You mean...as in inside?"

Summer holds her head. She had the most terrible headache. She had been in bed all day and had no plans of getting out.

"Summer!" she heard her dad shout from downstairs, "your friend's at the door!"

And so Leila comes back, Summer thinks. She had a nasty day yesterday at the well. No one knew about it except that leather book with Kokopelli on the cover. By the time she got up and across the hogan, her father was closing the door and locking flap and sealing it shut.

"Well? Was Leila there?"

Her father looked at her, "It was some boy. He dropped this off." In his hands was the black notebook with the skull and crossbones on the cover.

"Luke!" Summer shouts, hanging out of the tipi flap.

From down the street, he turns, "What?"

"Come back!"

*****

"Have you ever danced with the devil at the pale of moonlight?"

Summer Wind Serenade

"What?" Luke spills his cocoa.

"I'm sorry! That was in my head today. I don't know where it came from."

"Oh. Well, let's get some inspiration," Luke says, looking into Summers eyes.

"Shh, My father will hear!" Summer giggles.

Why do we sound drunk? Summer wonders, but totally abandons the thought. She was terribly glad that she had gotten him inside. Now to tell him that she liked him. "Luke, I..."

"Summer?"

"I..."

"Summer, I think you're going to pass out again."

*****

"Summer, I want you to tell me everything. Do not leave anything out, please."

And there Summer sat, on yet another brown leather bag. Except this time it was in front of a psychiatrist.

"Who are you?"

"I'm Dr. White. Your father has told me you have been passing out lately with no recollection of it occurring. So please tell me what's going on, and maybe we can find out what it is that makes you faint."

"I know what it is, doctor."

"Tell me...."

"It's this boy at my school."

Summer Wind Serenade

"What's his name? Details, Summer, details."

"His name is Luke. He's gorgeous."

"Luke? What does he look like?"

"Brown hair, strange eyes lighter than most. I never got a good look at them, but nice, he looks sweet."

"What school?"

Summer sighed. The thought of Luke went through her mind once more. "Just some high school."

*****

"It's not surprising you father sent you to a psychiatrist. You really have been acting strange lately."

"Well! Look who's talking!"

"Exactly!" Leila says, holding the shiny red apple.

"You know I got sent for fainting. The sad thing is, I fainted in front of the shrink too."

"And so? What's the verdict?" Leila asks, leaning forward.

Summer looks at her. She didn't want to tell her, and didn't want her to know anything about it.

"Excuse me," Summer says, standing up, "I have to dump Coyote."

"Is that it? Is that the reason you've been acting so strange?" Leila asks, completely full of doubt.

Summer becomes quiet, but she still walks to Coyote. Her heart is jumping when she sees Luke with them.

"Coyote," Summer begins, "we need to talk."

Summer Wind Serenade

Coyote looks at his group of friends, all of which are winking and whistling. Some of them are shouting inappropriate catcalls.

"Yes, what is it, angel?" Coyote asks, approaching Summer.

"We need to break up."

Coyote, looking at her slowly, peculiarly, does nothing for a few seconds. Summer stares back at him. Realizing she's serious, he grabs her and pulls her into an embracing kiss. He holds here there. As he lets her go, he stares into her eyes, searching.

Summer shakes her head sadly, "I'm sorry."

"Shit," is all he says after a moment. He's still staring at her. He then turns around and walks away.

"Shit, shit, shit, shit," Summer hears him say to himself. Summer and Leila are both silent.

"You're such a bitch!" Leila says after a minute, "You're such a total bitch."

And then Leila walked away.

*****

It was after-school and Summer was in Miss Long Trees classroom. She had passed out again that day, and Miss Long Tree had heard all about it through the student body's grapevine.

"Well! At least it wasn't in my class this time, eh? You keep doing a good job, alright? You'll get in that contest somehow or other! And you too, Mr. Luke!"

68

Summer Wind Serenade

Miss Long Tree smiles.

Luke just sits at his desk, his head down, and doesn't even want to see what's staring at him. Miss Long Tree is making a very frightening face.

"You know, the peculiar thing about you, Summer, is that when you're passed out, you speak!" Miss Long Tree whispers, her eyes wide open. "It's actually a tad spooky." She then walks out the door.

"I speak?" Summer wonders, staring at the doorway.

"Yes, you do speak," Luke says, not looking at her. He reaches in his bag and gets out a black notebook with a picture of a skull and crossbones on the cover.

"How do you know?" Summer asks, getting out her own Kokopelli notebook.

"Because whenever you faint, you say a bunch of stuff. And you're out for a few minutes, but then you come back, not remembering anything. It is pretty strange. It happened the other day on the horse, at your house, during class. It basically happens every day."

Summer looks out of the window.

"It's okay though," Luke added, "I'm getting used to your talking."

"What do I say? When I am out?" Summer asks, her heart pounding.

She hoped to God she didn't tell him. She prayed he didn't know she secretly crushed him, that he was her reason for living, breathing, writing every single line of every single poem that Miss Long Tree thought was priceless. But she sees Luke blush slightly and her heart suddenly stops. Summer falls backwards and hits her head on the desk behind her.

"Oh no," Summer whispers. She wanted to die from embarrassment. "Did I really?"

Luke just laughs. "Yea."

"I'm sorry."

"It's okay. Really. I did say I was used to it, didn't I?" Luke whispers.

Summer looks up, terrified. "It can't be," she whispers, feeling another cranial blackout coming on.

"Yes," he adds, still writing, "it's happened more than once."

*****

"What happens when you dream of him, Summer?" Dr. White asks.

"Nothing really. All I remember is one where we had four arms or something weird like that."

"And what were you thinking when you woke up?"

"I was thinking, it wouldn't matter if he had four arms, I would still like him."

"I see. Do you know Luke's last name? Does it hold any significance to you?"

"No. I have no idea what is last name is."

"Well, try and find out more for me, please. It could really be important. Okay, that's it. See you

Summer Wind Serenade

tomorrow, Summer."

*****

The next day during lunch, in Miss Long Tree's classroom, Summer waited silently, for Luke to show up. He was about five minutes later than usual. When he did show up, he looked tired.

"Oh my God, did you get any sleep last night?" Summer immediately asks.

"Not really."

He then sat down and began writing, Summer watching silently. When he finished, he handed it to her. Summer didn't read the poem first, she scrolled to the end and looked at his name.

"Written by Luke Whitewater." Now where had she heard that name? Had she heard it before? Or was it just a crazy memory?

"Are you going to read the entire thing?"

"Oh yeah, okay," Summer says, feeling stupid.

But while she read it, she didn't understand it because she kept thinking. *Luke Whitewater. Whitewater? Who's that?*

"Huh?" Summer jumps slightly.

"Summer, please wake up."

"I'm sorry, I had something on my mind."

"Okay, great."

Now I know his name, Summer thought to herself.

Summer Wind Serenade

"You're a full blood, aren't you? Or of that descent?"

"Yes, why?"

"Just making sure. Okay, did you find out Luke's last name?"

"Yes, Luke Whitewater."

"Great. You've been dreaming about my wife's son."

Summer looked at his name tag.

Dr. White.

"Uh....Dr. White, I'm so sorry!"

"It's quite alright. You know, if he's my son, I can find some things out for you. Truly."

Summer looks at him. *Was he for real?*

"It'll be easy. Tomorrow I'll tell you what I find out. Okay. Lets cut this appointment short. That's it, have a safe trip home, Summer."

*****

"Um, Luke?"

He looks up at Summer, he had been writing for the past ten minutes, silently.

"What does your father do for a living?"

Luke looks back down at his paper. "He's a psychiatrist... why?"

Summer looks out of the window. He was telling

Summer Wind Serenade

the truth after all. She had doubted it secretly, but now she knew for sure.

*****

"Right, Summer. I didn't really find anything out. But I did, however, find a paper from his notebook. It's about you, and maybe you should read it."

Later, when Summer got home, she read it. Her heart pounded, she wanted to know what was on it.

"today I had to work with her again. that summer. yeah I'm nice to her, but she can get really annoying. i hate how she faints all the time. especially the 'i love you' bit. what a faker. people call her a bitch, and I think they're right because she doesn't seem to care about anyone but herself. they also call her racist names behind her back because she's a full blood. don't get me wrong, i like indians and all other people, but her .. *long groan* no. she comes to miss long tree's classroom to tell me that she loves me and thinks that maybe there's a chance for us? not even. just looking at her makes me want to slap her, and I'll keep being nice as long as she keeps her distance and doesn't try anything ~Luke"

She read it over. Summer couldn't understand. She was sure that he liked her. How can this be? How

73

Summer Wind Serenade

could her first love not like her? And was everyone calling her a bitch and saying racist things about her? Why? She didn't do anything. She knew Leila probably hated her for personal reasons, and maybe even Coyote and his friends, but not Luke.

I'm going to forget about him,
I'm going to, I promise.
Ever since, it's been nothing
but heartache and loneliness.
For nothing.

My feelings have been crushed
my heart stabbed
my body repressed,
my emotions smashed...

"Yes, today is the day I forget about Luke. Leila doesn't know anything about him, and I'm not going to tell her.. yes, she knows who he is, but still. I'm not telling her."

Summer put down her diary, she didn't want to write in it anymore. She was going to stop dreaming, and live her life. "Goodbye, Luke. If I never see you again, I'll live happy and long, I'll be smart and beautiful once more."

But still, she felt the same. Her heart ached painfully. She still couldn't believe what Luke had said

Summer Wind Serenade

about her.

*****

"Miss Long Tree, I'm sorry, I can't come in anymore during lunch or after-school."

Miss Long Tree's face dropped.

"Why?"

"I have dance practice, and I need to rehearse."

"Well, I'm sorry to hear that. I'll miss you even though I didn't see you for that long. Farewell, Summer."

"Am I doing the right thing?" Summer asks herself, "Yes. Yes I am. No more, I can't do this. Out of sight, out of mind right?

And as the week went on, she would see him every now and then, but didn't say anything. She didn't want to think about it, she would forget him eventually. But still her heart ached and ached. Until one day, a week after she stopped showing up to Miss Long Tree's class, he finally approached her.

"So.. Summer, how come I don't see you after-school anymore?"

Summer hated him. She couldn't believe he was actually talking to her still. "You little idiot, leave me alone!" Summer shouts angrily, "You racist man!"

At that, everyone around her stopped.

"Summer! What is going on?" Miss Long Tree gasps, running over to her.

Summer Wind Serenade

"He calls me names behind my back!" Summer screams, pointing at Luke.

Luke just shook his head, his eyes wide.

"Luke! Is this true?" Miss Long Tree asks, slightly glaring.

"No," he says.

"He's a liar too!"

Summer couldn't take it. She ran off and kept running, not stopping. Her heart was still beating fast and it hurt more that ever. As she got home, she couldn't stop crying over and over. She could only imagine what people said about her.

"That bitch."

"She's so Indian, it's disgusting."

"The little Crazy Horse lover."

And these names went on and on in her mind. She couldn't stop them from coming. She read his paper over and over, and it made her worse. Her dream boy had called her a name.

"Forget him for calling me names," she repeated to herself miserably.

She was going to stop thinking about him. The only way she could was through sleep, and that would only bring him back into vision. So she could only think of one thing.

She walked into her fathers room, slowly. Her feet moving across the lush grass softly. She reached inside his chest and found his pack of cigarettes. And one by one, she went through them, her room a cloud of smoke, but she couldn't stop. She looked for more and more until the entire hogan smelled of smoke.

"Summer! What are you doing?" Her father was standing in front of her, gazing angrily, until she told him what happened.

He then held her and told her a story, about what happened to him when he was young. About how everyone hated him and his parents because they were full blood Native people. Why they weren't allowed in certain stores, why the police constantly harassed them, searching for a reason to jail them. And why his friends in school would suddenly stop talking to him without reason.

And then he told her about Jessica. The beautiful girl in the eleventh grade who he loved. How she just ignored him one day after he told her he was full blooded Native, and that was it. He decided that very day that he was leaving. He went to the reservation, and stayed there for a year, when one day, while he was at the ranchera, he saw her. He couldn't stop staring at the beautiful girl behind the counter. She was a full blood Native too, and had the looks of a goddess.

They married, had Summer, but then one day, she died. And he never got over her. Every day, he thought about her. Everything reminded him of her. And that was why he wasn't close to Summer. She looked too much like her mother, and he couldn't take it. When he was finished, they were both crying, and it made Summer feel better that maybe she wasn't the only person going

Summer Wind Serenade

through this. There were millions more before her, and millions of other racist people like Luke.

"You don't have to go back," her father said to her gently.

Summer looked at the grass. She didn't want to go. This was it, she couldn't go back. Especially after what happened. But still, something was telling her to go. Something unknown.

*****

"I heard what happened. And I'm really sorry. Whoever said it was a total jerk."

Summer hugged Leila. They were finally friends again.

During lunch, they sat together. Summer, Leila and the tiny red apple.

"Summer, are you alright?" Miss Long Tree began, "don't worry about what happened. Our school doesn't tolerate racism at all. Luke was sent to a different school."

Summer looks at her. Did she hear her right?

"Yes, Luke was sent to a different school for what he called you. Don't worry. It's far from here. But you shouldn't be in the poetry contest anymore. If he makes the final cut for his school, there's a large chance you'll see him there. So no more pressure about this contest from me, ok?"

Summer smiles weakly. Miss Long Tree was so good to her, she wondered why she had hated her. She

Summer Wind Serenade

was only trying to protect her.

"Thanks, Miss Long Tree," she says to her sincerely.

Miss Long Tree nods, smiles encouragingly, and walks away.

Summer couldn't think. She hated Luke so much for calling her the names that he did. But still, she remembered. "If Luke had four arms, I'd still love him."

All day, she tried not to cry, but it was hard. Everyone was paying more attention to her and telling her that they were there if she wanted to talk. Coyote approached her the next day. When she saw him, she realized she missed him. They hugged, and he kissed her cheek softly.

"I think you're cute," he whispers in her ear, "so forget what he said."

They walked around for a while that day, holding hands, but Summer still thought about Luke. She kept glancing at the Tree to see if he was standing there, staring at her. But he wasn't.

They spent that New Moon together. It had been an entire year since she first saw Luke. The time had gone by fast. Summer had cooked dinner for Coyote that evening. They were both 17. They ended reading her poetry. Coyote didn't react at all throughout the entire thing. But Summer remembered how Luke was when he was reading it.

"Coyote, do you love me?" Summer asks him finally.

Summer Wind Serenade

Coyote looks at her, thinking. And then he replies. "Yes, you're beautiful."

"Do you promise to love me forever?"

Coyote looks out of the window, thinking once more, "If I promise that, what will you promise me?"

Summer was silent, and started to cry, slowly. Coyote walked to her, and held her gently. It was almost midnight on New Moon, and she had had the worst year. What did she have to promise? It seemed like everything was taken away from her.

She stared at Coyote, he looked beautiful at that moment. Coyote looked at her, staring at her eyes for a moment. He knew she was serious. But he knew something else was wrong. It didn't seem like she was talking to him.

What was Luke doing at that same moment?

But she never saw Luke again.

Summer, all this time, had been reading her diary. Her eyes were filled with tears all over again. She had forgotten how much had happened.

"Oh God," she whispers softly. She had hoped all this time that the pain would of gone away. But it hadn't. What happened with her and Coyote was two weeks ago. He had left his sweater on her chest. Summer looks at his sweater, and sees something under it. A piece of paper. She gets up, and pulls it out from underneath.

"POETRY AND DANCE CONTEST!"

Come to the Indian Schools Poetry Reading and Dance Contest. Finalists from many schools will

Summer Wind Serenade

compete for:

    1st Place: $500 Scholarship

    2nd Place: $250 Scholarship

    3rd Place: $50 Scholarship

    First place will be submitted into the State Poetry and Dance competition.

    The event will take place on Wednesday, January 14, at dusk.

    Refreshments will be served. All are welcome!

    Summer looked at the paper again. She wondered if Luke would be there. She still missed him.

*****

    "Hey angel!"

    "Hi. I'm not feeling well. I'm sorry."

    "Oh, okay. It's alright. See ya."

    Summer closed the flap and she watched Coyote walking down the street.

    "I don't like him," she heard her father say.

    "Well, at least I didn't pick someone racist, daddy. He loves me."

    "They always love you at that age. Watch him, when he gets what he wants, he'll walk away and never come back."

    Her father then left. He would be gone all week. She would be alone again. She walked up to her mat and looked at the calender.

    January 14th.

Summer Wind Serenade

And on the calender was a little note from her father. It read. Page 34.

Page 34? Page 34 of what? She turned the paper over.

"Page 34 of the leather Kokopelli book."

Summer began to think. *What did he want her to know from her own diary?* But she got out her diary and counted up to page 34.

There, tucked inside, was another note from her father, with the paper that Luke had wrote about her. The paper read"

"Read this page of your diary"

Summer read it.

"Dear Diary:
Today, I read one of Luke's poems. He's such a good poet, I love his way of thinking. I especially love the way he writes. He seems to love capital letters because he writes a lot of his poems in capitals. I asked him, and he said he absolutely hated lower-case letters. Never in his life would he write a poem with all lover-cases. I especially love the way he writes his m's! The little arches! and oh-my God, his I's! Those are gorgeous! Well, that's it for today."

Summer looked over the entry again. She didn't get what her father was trying to say. She turned the page and there was one of Luke's poems.

Summer Wind Serenade

It was the one on death, "Oh my God," Summer whispers, not believing her eyes. "OH MY GOD!"

She looked at the page Luke wrote. The one that said he hated her. It was entirely lower-case, and the m's and I's were messy. This wasn't Luke's handwriting. Summer kept running and running. Her breath felt like it would give up on her, but she had to make it to school. She finally got there, the sun was disappearing, and the Poetry and Dance contest had already started.

As she walked in and sat down, there was an old lady on stage, speaking loudly, "Let's all give a big round of applause to Our Senior representatives! Now for Our Juniors!"

The audience applauded. Summer saw Luke sitting with a group of other contestants. She noticed several people from her own school.

"Our first reader for the Juniors is.." the old lady reached inside a hat and pulled out a name. The audience laughed, she looked ridiculous. Was she reaching for a bunny?

"Luke Whitewater!" the old lady boomed.

"Go Luke!" heard someone shout from the audience. It sounded a lot like her psychiatrist. Luke looked incredibly nervous. He stood at the microphone for a moment, his legs shaking terribly. But then he started.

"Our season by Luke Whitewater

Summer Wind Serenade

'My tears hit the pavement
My heart is now dead
Still shaking in pain
From everything you said

We sat together
And became one each day
From the glittering leaves of August
To the sparkling dew of May

And still I'm lonely
Forever aching for you
Hoping that you love me
And secretly ache for me too

I did nothing wrong
I promise that for you now
But still you're so far away
And my heart I still endow

So I go to bed every night
And wish on a star you'll come
From the bottom of my broken heart I say
And all the beauty of the rising sun

And I hope you'll realize someday soon
As a new season begins
I'll love you forever and ever
And Our season shall never end'

Summer Wind Serenade

As he finishes reading, his dad immediately stands up and begins shouting. Summer looks around, several others stand up as well. But she can't count how many, because her eyes are covered by tears. She had no idea what was going on as she went on hating Luke that entire time.

"Summer! So glad you could come!"

Summer looks and sees Miss Long Tree walking to her. She sits down beside her.

"But, why are you crying? Did you want to read a poem also?"

"I'm in love with Luke," Summer blurts out, still crying.

Miss Long Tree stares at her. She was completely frightened. "He hates you," was all she said, and she wraps her arms around her.

"No, Miss Long Tree. He didn't say any of that stuff. It was all fake. A lie!"

"Oh no," she whispers, "and I had him transferred and everything!"

Summer got up, walked by Miss Long Tree and went backstage. She had to find Luke. And there he was, standing in front of her.

"I love you," she said, and wrapped her arms around his neck.

"I thought you hated me," he whispered.

Summer started to laugh.

"I thought you hated me too!"

Summer Wind Serenade

"But why did you think that?"

Summer reached inside her pocket and pulled out the piece of paper. She handed it to him. His eyes grew wide as he read it.

"I know who wrote this," he starts, "it was my dad."

"But why would he do that?" Summer asks terrified.

"Because his family was part of Custers last stand. When your people slaughtered Custers men. My father still believes that Custer was right and you were wrong. He feels so strongly about it that he still carries the belief on today. And what he didn't tell you is that I am 1/4 Native too. My mother never told him that she was Native until after I was born, when it was too late to divorce her. He hates me, and that's why he denies being my father. Dr. White is my father. His last name is White, my mothers name is Whitewater. That's why I go by hers. And that's why I was the lightest and Indian school. I'm not full like you or Coyote or Leila." Luke shuddered.

"And that's it? That's why he hates me now? That's why he tried to keep us apart?"

Luke opens his mouth to reply but then stops. His father is staring directly behind Summer.

"Of course that's why I hate you, you little bitch. I despised you the moment I saw you," whispers Dr. White in pure hatred, "I hate you all, all you people!"

Summer looks at Luke, both of them petrified

Summer Wind Serenade

with terror.

"When you were in my office," Dr. White continues, "I wanted to strangle you for what you did to me and my family. You ruined my family you little bitch!"

Summer stares at him. He had a glistening look of insanity in his eyes. For a moment Dr. White glares at Summer.

"I'm going to kill you," he then whispers, breathing loudly. And then that's when she noticed it. She looks at Luke. He noticed it too. On stage, it was entirely quiet. Was there an echo? "Yes, I'm going to kill all of you useless good for nothing wastes of air! Starting with you! You little bitch!" Dr. White shrieks, lunging at her.

Suddenly the door backstage slams open. Several police officers run in, holding guns in front of them.

"Freeze!" They creep closer and handcuff Dr. White, who is suddenly calm again. His hair is completely out of place.

"Excuse, me officer, but is there a problem?"

"Don't play dumb. Someone left the mikes on back here. We heard everything, you racist pig." They take him away.

"Summer! Luke! are you two alright?" Miss Long Tree cries, running to them. She looks completely terrified, as if Dr. White had been screaming at her instead of at them. "It's okay, it's okay," she whispers gently, holding them. It sounded like she was trying to

Summer Wind Serenade

calm herself down more than them.

"Yeah, we're okay," Luke says.

"Yea," Summer agrees.

"Okay," Miss Long Tree sighs. "Whew. What an episode. I reckon I won't be able to sleep for a week! Oh, and Luke! I will talk to the district about bringing you back, alright?"

Luke nods, grinning. Miss Long Tree smiles comfortingly at Summer.

"You keep writing, okay? I'm dying to hear your reply to Luke's poem!"

Summer blushes deep red, and both Miss Long Tree and Luke laugh loudly. Miss Long Tree walks away from them.

Luke clears his throat and speaks, "Well, Summer, looks like my dad won't be coming back for a while. So why don't you live with me?"

Summer blushes once more. "I'll think about it. For now, let's just get out of here."

And then they walk happily, hand in hand. The beautiful Summer and her gorgeous boyfriend Luke.

*****

And Leila started eating more. She no longer brought the tiny apple to school, no, she started bringing a real lunch. Once she recovered her figure, and was no longer a skinny girl, and Coyote immediately noticed. He dropped Summer and went for Leila instead.

Summer Wind Serenade

The nurse worked at the school for the rest of her life. She still scolded Summer every time she saw her, "Don't be doing drugs in this town, girl!"

And Coyotes' friends, the whistling bunch, ended up dropping Summer, finally. If you want to meet them, you'll find them at the Tree drooling over every girl passing by. They go there every night.

Summer's father totally approves of her and Luke's relationship. In a separate chest, you can probably find a whole load of baby clothes, toys and money. He's planning ahead.

And for Summer and Luke, they got married.

*****

The banners shined beautifully, hung from two pillars.

CONGRATULATIONS!

Summer was so happy, she had made it. She had grown so much, and she couldn't believe how much had happened. Today was her wedding day.

Throughout the reception, everyone came up to Summer and Luke to wish them good luck. Leila, Coyote, all of Coyotes' friends, Miss Long Tree, all their teachers and everyone from Lukes family, with exception to his father, were there.

"Congratulations," says Leila, "I'm glad you married Luke!"

Summer knew she was really glad. Because now

Summer Wind Serenade

she had Coyote to herself. If only he would notice her.

"I'm sure Coyote will come around," Summer assures her.

"I'm sure too," Leila smiles.

"Well, my darling, we're off!" Luke shouts happily. He opens the door to the wedding caravan (which was a white carriage) and Summer climbs in.

"Wait!" Leila shouts, "Wait! Summer! You forgot to throw the bouquet!" Leila then looks at Coyote, determined to catch it.

Summer climbs back out and turns around. Her heart is beating fast. She throws it in the air, and at once, she hears girls shrieking and screaming. She turns around to see who caught it. Leila is standing there, holding it. She looks around, dazed at first, but then she smiles grandly and points at Coyote.

Summer and Luke climb back into their carriage and it begins moving. Summer looks out at the crowd, and waves goodbye to everyone, Luke doing the same. She notices her father in particular, is completely overjoyed. Coyote and Leila are kissing desperately, as if holding on to each others lips for dear life.

"Goodbye, Leila! Goodbye, Coyote!" Summer shouts. As they went on, Summer smiles at Luke, "So, where are we going?"

"We're going to the stars!" he grins happily.